Monty the
Sad Puppy

Other titles by Holly Webb

The Snow Bear

The Reindeer Girl

The Winter Wolf

The Storm Leopards

The Snow Cat

Animal Stories:

Lost in the Snow

Alfie all Alone

Lost in the Storm

Sam the Stolen Puppy

Max the Missing Puppy

Sky the Unwanted Kitten

Timmy in Trouble

Ginger the Stray Kitten

Harry the Homeless Puppy

Buttons the Runaway Puppy

Alone in the Night

Ellie the Homesick Puppy

Jess the Lonely Puppy

Misty the Abandoned Kitten

Oscar's Lonely Christmas

Lucy the Poorly Puppy

Smudge the Stolen Kitten

The Rescued Puppy

The Kitten Nobody Wanted

The Lost Puppy

The Frightened Kitten

The Secret Puppy

The Abandoned Puppy

The Missing Kitten

The Puppy Who was Left Behind

The Kidnapped Kitten

The Scruffy Puppy

The Brave Kitten

The Forgotten Puppy

The Secret Kitten

A Home for Molly

Sammy the Shy Kitten

The Seaside Puppy

The Curious Kitten

Maisie Hitchins:

The Case of the Stolen Sixpence

The Case of the Vanishing Emerald

The Case of the Phantom Cat

The Case of the Feathered Mask

The Case of the Secret Tunnel

The Case of the Spilled Ink

The Case of the Blind Beetle

The Case of the Weeping Mermaid

Monty the Sad Puppy

Holly Webb

Illustrated by Sophy Williams

For everyone who asked for another Labrador book!

www.hollywebbanimalstories.com

STRIPES PUBLISHING
An imprint of the Little Tiger Group
1 The Coda Centre, 189 Munster Road,
London SW6 6AW

A paperback original
First published in Great Britain in 2017

Text copyright © Holly Webb, 2017
Illustrations copyright © Sophy Williams, 2017
Author photograph copyright © Nigel Bird

ISBN: 978-1-84715-773-7

A CIP catalogue record for this book is available
from the British Library.

Printed and bound in the UK.

10 9 8 7 6 5 4 3 2 1

Chapter One

"Shall we head down to the field now?"
Amelie suggested. "Then we can give
Monty a really good run." She laughed.
"Look, he heard me!"

Monty's soft black ears had
suddenly pricked up and he was
staring hopefully at Amelie. He was
only a puppy but he already had long
Labrador legs and he loved to run.

Her brother checked the time on his phone. "Yeah, OK, but not for too long. We've already been out twenty minutes and he's only supposed to walk for about twenty-five."

Amelie sighed. "I know the leaflet said that but look at him, Josh! He's desperate! He wants a proper run, don't you, Monty?"

The little black Labrador frisked round her feet with an excited bark. "It's just not fair, is it? You love walks so much and so do we!"

Amelie crouched down to rub his head and run his ears through her fingers. His ears were so silky, and she loved the way he closed his eyes and stuck his nose in the air every time she did it.

"Well, it won't be that long till he can go on really big walks," Josh said and then grinned. "He's already five months old – so that's only another seven months to go!"

Amelie rolled her eyes. Josh thought he was so funny sometimes – she and Mum reckoned it was a teenage boy thing. "Come on, Josh, pleeease? If we go to the field then we can take the alley and go the quick way home."

When they'd first got Monty, three months earlier, the breeder had given them a leaflet of tips on how to look after a Labrador puppy properly. She'd explained that Monty couldn't go out for walks at all till he'd had his vaccinations. And even then, they'd have to be careful not to overwalk him while he was still under a year. The information leaflet suggested a five-minute rule – only five minutes of proper exercise for every month of Monty's age, so as not to injure his growing legs.

Amelie knew it was the right thing to do but she still didn't like it. Their walks seemed to have hardly got going before they had to turn round again.

"I suppose…" Josh agreed. "At least he'll be nice and hungry for his dinner. Come on then, Monty! Let's go to the field!"

Monty pranced along happily. He loved going out in the afternoons with Amelie and Josh. In the morning he went out with their dad, who did too much stopping to chat to people while he walked round the lake. Amelie and Josh raced about and threw sticks, and they usually brought toys for him to chase. He pulled eagerly at his lead, making for the gate out to the field.

"Heel, Monty," Amelie said, pulling him back gently. She and Josh had been taking Monty to puppy training classes, and they'd been told not to let him pull when they were walking to heel.

Monty dropped back obediently and Josh fumbled a treat out of his pocket. "Good dog!"

"You wouldn't think he'd only been going to training for three weeks, would you?" Amelie said proudly, as she opened the gate.

Josh grinned. "He's a greedy pig. He'll do anything for those treats."

"Yes, but some dogs never learn to do things like that. I mean, what about Daisy? Grandad can't ever get her to sit and stay, and she only walks to heel when she feels like it. Think about last week!"

"Yeah…" Josh shook his head, remembering. Grandad had come with them on a walk to the park with

Daisy, his little dachsund. They'd walked past a girl eating a biscuit and Daisy had nibbled it right out of her hand. Her mum had been really cross, even though Grandad had said sorry loads of times. He had felt awful about it but Daisy hadn't been bothered at all...

"I reckon that's because she's a dachshund, though," Josh pointed out. "They're not very easy to train. Labradors like Monty are good at this sort of thing. I mean, you don't ever get dachshund Guide Dogs, do you?"

Amelie giggled. "Daisy would be a useless Guide Dog. Maybe you're right about all Labs being good but I do think Monty's extra-clever. Here, you can take his lead for a bit, if you like."

Monty was staring up at them both hopefully, waiting for the chance to dash off into the field. Amelie patted his head, then passed the lead to Josh.

"Come on, Monty," she called, jogging backwards on to the long grass around the edge of the football pitch.

Amelie loved Newland Park. She remembered going there when she was tiny. Dad had taken her for walks round the lake almost every day and let her throw food to the ducks. But it was only now they had a dog that she realized how lucky they were to have the park so close by. All the houses in their street backed on to it.

Josh and Monty raced past Amelie, Monty barking and yipping with excitement. She ran after them and then stopped to look through the wire fence as she reached their back garden. Sometimes Dad came out to drink a cup of tea if he was having a break from work. She peered past the apple tree, trying to see further up the garden, but he wasn't there. She waved, just in case, before chasing after her brother and Monty. The puppy was so excited that he was dashing around in circles.

"Watch out, Josh!" Amelie cried but it was too late.

Monty had seen Amelie coming and decided to race towards her, pulling the lead tight around Josh's legs and yanking his feet out from under him. Her tall, skinny brother fell like a tree, collapsing into the long grass with a groan.

"Catch him!" he called. "Amelie! The lead!"

"I've got it!" Amelie yelled, snatching at Monty's trailing lead as he danced around her. "Here, Monty. You silly dog," she said lovingly. "What did you think you were doing, hmm?"

"I'm fine, thank you for asking," Josh muttered, heaving himself up out of the grass. "Uuurgh. I think I landed in something disgusting."

Amelie peered at the brown patch down the side of Josh's jeans. "It's only mud," she said reassuringly. "You are OK, aren't you?"

"Yes." Josh sighed. "No thanks to you, Monty. Well, I'll know not to let him wind me up in the lead like that again. I wouldn't have thought he was that strong!"

Monty sat at Amelie's feet, gazing

up at them both and panting happily.
He had no idea what Josh was talking
about but he was hoping it didn't mean
the end of the walk.

Amelie had thought Josh would be
able to sneak upstairs and change
before Dad spotted him when they got
home. But their dad was in the hallway
when they returned – and so was
Mum, which was really unusual. She
was hardly ever home early from the
shop where she worked.

   Amelie unclipped Monty's lead and
he dashed off to the kitchen for a drink
of water. Mum gave Amelie a hug but
Amelie looked up at her anxiously –

she had a serious expression on her face.

"What's wrong?" Josh asked, forgetting about his jeans.

Mum took a deep breath. "It's Grandad..." she started and Amelie's stomach clenched. Their mum's dad hadn't been well for a while. A few months ago he'd had a stroke and been in hospital for a few days. But Amelie thought he'd been getting better now he was back at home again. He'd seemed fine when they'd last seen him.

"What's happened?" she whispered, her eyes suddenly hot with tears.

Mum put an arm round her shoulders. "It's another stroke. Don't panic, Amelie, it looks like he'll be all right. But it's going to take longer for him to recover this time. He's probably not going to be able to look after himself at home, even once he's allowed out of hospital. He'll need to be in a nursing home for a bit, where there are staff who can help."

"Oh…" Amelie leaned against her, relieved. For a moment she'd thought Mum was going to give them much worse news. "Poor Grandad," she said.

Josh frowned. "Do you mean he'll always need to be looked after, Mum?"

"We're not sure." Mum and Dad exchanged a worried look. "It's only just happened, Josh. I haven't even been to see him yet. But from what the hospital said, it's more serious this time. Grandad will probably have to move permanently to some sort of sheltered housing. Somewhere there's lot of support."

"What's going to happen to Daisy?" Amelie asked, looking up. "Will Grandad be able to take her with him?"

Mum stared at her. "Oh my goodness. I'd forgotten about Daisy. Grandad's neighbours fed her the last time he was in hospital."

Dad ran his hand through his hair. "That's not going to work this time, though. She's going to need a proper home." He looked thoughtfully round the hallway, as though he was imagining another dog trotting down it. Amelie caught her breath.

"Your mum and I talked about this a while ago," Dad went on. "After all, Daisy already knows us, doesn't she?"

Mum nodded. "We mentioned it to Grandad, too. That Daisy could come and live here with us."

Monty wandered back into the hallway, looking curiously at them all still standing there. Amelie crouched down to stroke him and he nuzzled against her, licking her cheek. Amelie thought maybe he could taste that she'd been crying. His tail was waving, just a little, the way it did when he was worried.

"Oh, Monty…" Amelie murmured. "How would you feel about sharing your home with another dog?"

Chapter Two

"So you're going to have two dogs?"
Ella asked, leaning across the table to
whisper. "You're so lucky, Amelie, I
don't even have one! Is Daisy cute?"

Amelie nodded. "She's a gorgeous
colour – russet, Grandad calls her, and
her coat's so glossy, even shinier than
Monty's. She's tiny but she thinks
she's in charge. She's always bossing

my grandad around!" Then she sighed. "He's going to miss her so much – I mean, he's had Daisy for eight years. I'm really excited about looking after her and it's going to be great for Monty, having a friend at home all the time. But I wish Daisy could stay with Grandad."

"I'm sorry he's in hospital, Amelie," Ella said. "But I bet he's happy you'll be looking after Daisy."

"Mum told Grandad we'd go and get her today. Dad's going to pick me up from school in the car, then we'll go straight over to the house."

"Are you two actually discussing the Romans?" Miss Garrett asked, leaning over Amelie's shoulder and making her jump.

"Um. We were…" she muttered. "Sorry, Miss Garrett."

"Sorry, Miss Garrett," Ella repeated.

"Well, get on with it, girls. I'd like a plan drawn up by break time, please."

Ella sighed as their teacher moved on to the next table. "I wish we didn't always have to make things for topic work. My Viking ship last year was just embarrassing."

"What do you think you'll do this time?" Amelie asked. "What about a costume? You could make a Roman dress, if your mum wouldn't mind you using an old sheet." She flicked through the book they'd found in the school library. "Oh, wow… I'd like to make something like that!"

Ella peered at the mosaic picture of

a fierce-looking guard dog. "All those tiny squares! It'll take hours."

"It looks really fun. I could cut the squares out of craft foam."

Ella nodded. "I suppose so. Don't forget you're going to have two dogs to play with, though!"

Amelie nodded. "I haven't – I can't wait for this afternoon!"

Amelie picked up the dog carrier and walked carefully out to the car, murmuring soothingly to Daisy. She told the little dachshund how excited Monty would be when she arrived and how much fun they were all going to have.

Daisy had been really pleased to see them when they arrived at Grandad's house. Amelie thought she'd probably had a lonely sort of day, since she was used to having Grandad around most of the time. But she hadn't been keen on going in her carrier at all. She'd backed away from Amelie, her long ears shaking.

"Maybe she thinks we're taking

her to the vet," Dad suggested, as he unlocked the car.

"Shh, Dad! You know Grandad says she understands that word! You have to spell it out," Amelie reminded him.

"Oh, yes. Sorry, Daisy. Are you OK with the carrier on your lap, Amelie? Hold it tight."

Amelie wrapped her arms firmly around the carrier. There was no sound at all from inside but she could see Daisy through the holes in the plastic sides. The dachshund was standing up with her nose pressed against the wire door.

"Sit down, Daisy-dog," Amelie whispered, as Dad started the car. "You'll wobble." But Daisy stayed on her feet, even though the movement of the car made her lurch about. Amelie kept on whispering encouraging things but Daisy seemed too confused to sit down. She just kept on slipping from side to side, her little black claws scrabbling against the plastic floor of the carrier. The blanket Grandad kept in there was all scrunched up at the back. Daisy wasn't whining or yapping, which was really odd. Grandad always said she was the chattiest dog he'd ever met but now she was completely silent.

"Is she all right?" Dad asked, as they stopped at the lights.

"I don't know..." Amelie admitted.

"She looks really nervous. Maybe you're right and she does think she's going to the V–E–T."

Dad glanced over at the carrier, frowning. "We're nearly home. Not long now, Daisy."

Amelie stood on the doorstep, waiting for Dad to find his keys and looking at the hunched little dog inside the carrier. She wouldn't have minded so much if Daisy had howled all the way home. Amelie hurried into the house and put the carrier down in the hallway, just as Josh came out of the kitchen holding a half-eaten piece of toast. Monty raced after him, whining with excitement as he saw Amelie and Dad. Then he saw the carrier and skidded to a halt.

There was a skittering, scrabbling noise from inside and a low growl. Monty retreated behind Josh, his tail drooping. Amelie looked anxiously between the two dogs. Dad had said that they ought to introduce Daisy and Monty to each other slowly but Amelie hadn't thought it would be a problem. Monty had been to Grandad's house and Daisy had been coming to their house for years. Why wouldn't they be happy to see each other? Maybe it just wasn't the same without Grandad there, too.

"Shall we let Daisy out now?" she asked Dad.

Dad sighed. "Yes, I suppose we'd better. Let's keep her in the kitchen to start with. Josh, can you put Monty out in the garden? Let's give Daisy a bit of space."

"Uh-huh." Josh caught Monty's collar. The puppy was still staring at the carrier, looking confused. "Come on, Monty. Is Daisy OK? She's very quiet."

"She looks miserable," Amelie said. "Do you think she knows Grandad's ill?"

"I'm sure she knows *something*'s wrong…" Dad said. "Dogs are very good at sensing that sort of thing."

Monty peered round Josh's arm as Amelie picked up the carrier. What was going on? There was another dog in there, he could smell her. It was Daisy – he knew her. What was

Daisy doing in his house? And now Amelie was putting the carrier down in the kitchen, where his basket and his food bowl were.

He wriggled and pulled as Josh tried to unlock the back door, twisting and scrabbling so that Josh let go of him. Monty backed away clumsily, skidding on the tiles, and padded up to the carrier, sniffing hard. He stretched out one careful paw to the wire door, turning his head from side to side as he tried to work out what was going on.

There was a sharp yap from inside and Monty jumped back, tucking his tail between his legs. Then he crept forward, sniffing again. Daisy had always been friendly before. Monty's tail twitched slowly to and fro as he stared at her, confused.

"It's OK, Monty," Amelie said, gently pushing him away. "Josh's just taking you out so you don't upset Daisy, that's all."

"Come on, Monty." Josh took hold of the puppy's collar again and Monty squirmed, pulling away anxiously. Was he in trouble? This time Josh had a better grip and Monty couldn't get free. Josh let go of him outside the door and then ducked smartly back into the kitchen. Monty scampered after him

but the door clicked closed just in front
of his nose. Then he heard the sound of
the dog flap locking, too. Josh had shut
him out.

Monty stood staring at the door,
his ears flattened back. Why was he
stuck outside, while Daisy was in *his*
kitchen?

Monty pawed at the door, whining.
He wanted Amelie. He was getting
hungry, too, but mostly he wanted
Amelie to hold him and pat him, so
he knew that everything was all right.
Instead he was shut out in the garden.
It felt as though he'd been there
for ages.

He skittered back as the door opened suddenly and Amelie appeared. He whined – he'd been so desperate to get back in but now he wasn't sure what to do. He could smell Daisy inside – she was still there.

"Are you going to come in?" Amelie coaxed. "Come and see Daisy."

Monty looked past her into the doorway and spotted Daisy. She was sitting under the kitchen table, her head drooping. He looked up at Amelie, still unsure what was going on.

"It's just Daisy," Dad said, crouching down beside Monty. "You know Daisy." He glanced at Amelie and Josh. "This is a bit harder than I thought it would be. Let's feed them both – that should cheer them up."

Dad brought out Daisy's food and water bowls, and the big bag of dry food that Grandad used. It was the same kind that they gave Monty, Amelie noticed, except that it was for an older dog, not a puppy.

"Should we put their bowls close together?" Amelie asked. "Would that help?"

Dad shook his head. "Not yet. Let's work up to it. We'll put Daisy's over here, by the door."

Monty was looking happier now, wagging his tail eagerly as he saw his bag of food come out. But Daisy hadn't moved. She was still under the table and she wasn't paying any attention to the food Dad was pouring into her bowl. Amelie watched as

Monty wolfed down his dinner and
Daisy ignored hers completely.

"I suppose she doesn't feel like
eating," Josh said slowly, crouching
down by the table and reaching out
his hand for Daisy to sniff. But Daisy
turned her head away. "She's missing
him, isn't she? She knows things
aren't right."

"I really hope she cheers up soon," Amelie said. "What are we going to tell Grandad?"

Dad sighed. "I'm sure she'll settle down. We can't expect her to be happy straight away."

"I guess so," Amelie said. But she hadn't thought it would be like this. She'd imagined walks and cuddles with two gorgeous dogs. Instead she had a confused puppy and a miserable dog who wouldn't even eat.

Chapter Three

"It's all right, Monty." Amelie smoothed his ears gently. "It's going to be OK. I hope…" she added in a whisper.

She and Monty were sitting in the hallway on the bottom step. The two dogs didn't seem to be getting on very well. When they'd met before it had mostly been for walks – Amelie,

Josh and Grandad had loved going out together with the dogs. Somehow it was different now that they were sharing a house. Monty had gone up and tried to give Daisy a friendly sniff but she'd growled at him, showing her teeth, and he'd backed away, looking frightened. Amelie had decided to take Monty out of the room again and give Daisy some time to settle.

"Perhaps I should have guessed this would be confusing for you, too," Amelie muttered. "I just thought Daisy would keep you company while me and Josh were at school. Dad says you're always making sad eyes at him when he's working."

Monty leaned against Amelie's knees, enjoying the fuss she was making of him. His strange, bewildered feeling eased as she rubbed his ears. He let out a long huff of breath, his eyes half-closing.

"Ready to go, Amelie?" said Mum, walking down the stairs.

"Do I have to come?" Amelie asked, staring at Monty's ears so she didn't have to look at Mum.

"Don't you want to see Grandad?" Mum sat down on the stairs behind her. "He'd love to see you. Josh wanted to come but he's got football practice. Are you worried about going to the hospital, sweetheart? I don't think it'll be scary. Grandad's doing really well."

Amelie turned to look up at her. "It isn't that. I mean, maybe a bit but mostly I don't know what to say about Daisy. Grandad's going to ask us how she is and I don't want to tell him."

Mum put a hand on Amelie's shoulder. "Grandad's not going to expect miracles, Amelie. He'll know she's going to be upset to begin with. He's really pleased we're looking after her, you know. When I went to see him last night he said he knew you'd look after her for him."

"But I'm not looking after her!" Amelie sniffed hard and then half-laughed as Monty snuggled his damp nose against her chin. "Look – Monty can tell I'm worried. Daisy's so upset, Mum. She didn't eat dinner and she's really grumpy with Monty. I think she hates being here, full stop."

Mum nodded. "Wouldn't you, though? If you'd suddenly been taken to a new place, with people you didn't really know, and you didn't understand what was happening? And you were missing your best friend? She's only been here a couple of hours, Amelie. We've just got to give her time."

Grandad looked small, Amelie decided. That was what was so weird. He was a tall man but in the hospital bed he seemed to have shrunk.

"Ignore the pyjamas, Amelie," he said as she came in, grinning at her and trying to heave himself up against the pillows. "These horrible yellow things are from the hospital. Your mum's promised to nip back over to my house and get me my own ones."

Amelie giggled. "They are a funny colour," she agreed. Grandad looked really pale and washed out – she didn't think it was just because of the pyjamas but it was easier to pretend. "Are you feeling all right?" she asked, feeling slightly awkward.

"Just tired." Grandad reached out to pat her hand and Amelie moved closer to him – she could see how hard it was for him to lift his arm. She'd been hoping that he'd be able to come out of the hospital soon but now she could see how serious things were.

"How's Daisy?" Grandad asked. "How's Monty coping with her bossing him around? Is she being a little madam?"

Amelie swallowed. "A bit..." She wished Daisy *would* be bossy. That would be better than her being so quiet and unhappy.

"She's still getting used to the move, Dad," Amelie's mum put in. "I'm sure she'll be fine soon."

Grandad nodded but he looked worried.

"It'll be OK, Grandad," Amelie found herself saying. "I promise we'll make her happy."

"I know you will, love." Grandad smiled at her. "She's in good hands."

Amelie smiled, too, but behind her back she was digging her nails into her palms. How could they make Daisy happy when she was so upset? But now she'd made a promise. And she was going to do everything she could to keep it.

"Josh! Josh, wake up!"

"Amelie…" Josh groaned and pulled the duvet up around his ears. "What's the matter?"

Amelie perched on the edge of his bed and Monty snuffled his nose under Josh's duvet.

"Eugh! Cold," Josh moaned. "Get off, Monty."

"I need to talk to you. I've hardly slept at all, thinking about it."

"About what?" Josh sat up and looked at Amelie blearily. His hair was sticking up and he still seemed half-asleep.

"I need you to help me make Daisy
happy."

"What?" Josh yawned.

"I promised Grandad," Amelie
explained. "I didn't mean to, it just
came out. I wanted to cheer him up…
I told him we'd make Daisy happy.
So now we have to."

"Me?" Josh sighed.

"Both of us! What can we do? I've just been down to feed her and Monty, and she's still not eating. She had a tiny nibble of her biscuits and then went back to her basket. And I think Monty's scared of her. He kept looking over at her the whole time he was eating."

Josh ran his hands through his hair and sighed. "I wish the hospital let dogs in. She's missing Grandad and he's missing her. If only they could see each other."

Amelie nodded. "She's only little – do you think we could smuggle her in? Maybe in my school bag?"

Josh grinned. "I wish we could. But she'd bark her head off if we tried to put her in a bag. We might get banned from the hospital."

"I suppose so…" Then Amelie sat up, staring at him. "She can't *see* Grandad … but what about hearing him? We could phone him at the hospital and he can talk to Daisy!"

Josh nodded. "Yes! That's perfect, Amelie! Let's go and do it now."

Amelie jumped up but then she stopped. "I'm not sure we should, not before school. Grandad looked so tired yesterday – he might still be asleep." She sighed. "Let's call him when we get home. A few hours won't matter…" It just seemed such a long time for Daisy to wait.

Amelie spent the whole day worrying about Monty and Daisy. Dad had said that he'd try to take them both out for a morning walk but Amelie wasn't sure Daisy would want to go. She'd been out in the garden to wee but she hadn't seemed to enjoy the fresh air. She'd just trailed back into the house. When Monty wanted walks, he danced around her eagerly, or sometimes he sat in front of his lead, whining and trying to claw it off its hook. Daisy hadn't done anything like that.

"What's the matter?" Ella asked her at break time.

"Monty and Daisy aren't getting on," Amelie admitted. "I got so excited about having Daisy come to live with us, I didn't even think about what it would really be like."

Ella looked sympathetic. "But dogs do get new owners sometimes. I bet she'll get used to you soon."

"I hope so. We've got a plan, anyway." Amelie explained about the phone call and Ella nodded.

"That sounds like a great idea," she said, as the bell went. "Don't worry, Amelie. I'm sure hearing your grandad's voice will cheer Daisy up."

Amelie had promised to wait for Josh so they could phone Grandad together but he seemed to take hours to walk home from school that afternoon. She watched out for him from her bedroom window with Monty curled up on his cushion next to her.

Monty was supposed to sleep in the kitchen – he definitely preferred sleeping in Amelie's room, though. Mum and Dad had told Amelie he shouldn't sleep on her bed, because when he was fully grown there'd be no room for her. So he had a big cushion next to the bed instead.

As soon as Amelie saw her brother coming down the road, she leaped from the windowsill and galloped down the stairs. Monty had been half-asleep but he woke up as Amelie dashed past him. Where was she going? He blinked after her, confused, and then got up, shaking himself awake to follow her.

"OK, OK, I'm coming," Josh said, pulling his mobile out of his pocket as Amelie dragged him into the kitchen. The two baskets were still at opposite ends of the room – Daisy's little dachshund-sized one and the great big basket that Dad had bought for Monty to grow into.

"Dad said she wouldn't go for a walk this morning," Amelie told Josh. "She wouldn't even get out of her basket."

"Maybe this'll help," Josh said, searching for Grandad's number. Amelie crouched down next to Daisy, eyeing the little dog anxiously. She really hoped this would work.

Daisy was curled up in a ball, with one paw stretched over her muzzle – almost as if she was trying to cover her eyes. She'd obviously heard Amelie and Josh coming. She opened one dark eye and stared at them suspiciously.

"Josh! Amelie! Your mum told me about your idea!" Amelie could hear Grandad's voice, small and hollow sounding, from the phone.

"Hi, Grandad. I'm putting you on speaker – Daisy's right here."

Before Josh could even touch the screen, Daisy was on her feet, her ears as pricked as a dachshund's ever could be. Josh laughed. "Grandad, she can definitely hear you! Say hello to her!"

"Daisy! Oh, there's my lovely girl…"

Amelie blinked back sudden tears. She didn't really know why she was crying – it was just that Grandad sounded so happy to be talking to Daisy. Daisy looked happier, too. She had her nose pressed up against the phone and her tail was wagging the tiniest bit. It was working!

Amelie beamed at Josh and he grinned back at her.

Monty sat alone in the kitchen doorway, watching them fuss over Daisy, his head hanging low. As Amelie reached up to high-five Josh, he looked up eagerly, his tail starting to wag, hoping that she'd notice him. But Amelie was too busy watching Daisy.

Chapter Four

"Come on, Monty! Walk time!"

Monty raced down the hallway, almost crashing into Amelie's legs. He was desperate for a really good long walk.

It had been five days since Grandad had gone into hospital. Josh and Amelie had done their best but walks had taken second place to hospital visits. They'd even had to miss Monty's dog-training class on Saturday. But when they went to visit Grandad on Sunday he had told them to stop fussing. "I'm definitely on the mend," he told Amelie firmly. "You need to go home and spend some time with those dogs. Sunday afternoon's the perfect time for a long walk."

Monty ducked back as Daisy suddenly appeared from behind Amelie's feet. He was still nervous around her. Daisy didn't seem to care that she was so much smaller than he was. If he came near her food or her basket, she'd bare her teeth at him and growl. So Daisy was coming on the walk, too? He dropped back, crouching low and wagging his tail a little to try and show her that he was friendly.

"It's OK, Monty. Come on," Amelie said, holding out his lead. "We're going to the park – it'll be fun!"

"Ready to go? I'm looking forward to this." Dad came out of his office, rubbing his eyes. "I've been at the computer for too long." Dad was about to go away for a conference, so he was working all hours trying to get everything done before he went. "Josh, are you sure you're not coming?"

"Homework," Josh growled from upstairs.

Dad got Monty's lead and clipped it on, and Monty followed Amelie and Daisy out of the front door. He could tell from the way they turned that they were going down the alley to the back entrance of the park and his walk got bouncier. Were they going to the field? Maybe Amelie would run with him.

But then Dad led the way on to the path round the lake instead. Monty tugged at his lead, trying to pull towards the field, but Dad just said, "Heel, Monty," and kept going. Monty followed, looking back regretfully at the long grass in the field. It was a warm day and the grass looked so cool and inviting.

Lots of people came over to make a fuss of Daisy – the park was full of dog-walkers since it was a Sunday. They were mostly people who'd seen Amelie with Monty before and they wanted to hear about the new dog. Amelie and Dad kept stopping and starting, and Monty was bored. He felt all fidgety, as though his paws were itching. He wanted to chase something.

Dad was holding him on a loose lead while they chatted to a lady with a spaniel when a pigeon walked past, right in front of his nose. Monty felt so full of energy he couldn't resist. He leaped after it, barking loudly and almost pulling the lead out of Dad's hand. The pigeon fluttered away with an indignant batting of wings. Dad stumbled, caught off balance, and put his foot down heavily right next to Daisy's back paw. Daisy yapped sharply and cowered backwards in fright.

"Monty, no!" Dad snapped, pulling him back, and Monty hunched his shoulders apologetically. Wasn't he supposed to do that? He was just so sick of standing still.

The lady with the spaniel smiled sympathetically at Monty. "He looks like he wants to get going. Good luck with them both."

"I suppose we'd better get home." Dad sighed. "Haven't you got that project to get started on, Amelie?"

"Do we have to, Dad? We were going to go for a proper long walk."

"I know, but look at Daisy. Monty really scared her."

Amelie nodded sadly. Daisy was hiding behind Dad's legs, shivering. It wasn't fair to make her walk any more if she didn't want to. "OK. Come on, Monty."

Monty stared up at Amelie in surprise. They were going home? Already? Was it because he'd chased that bird? Reluctantly, he plodded after Dad – that had hardly felt like a walk at all.

"Daisy's definitely starting to settle in," Amelie told Ella when she saw her at school on Monday. "We got Grandad to talk to her on the phone a few times over the weekend and she looks a lot happier now. She even came out for a walk with us yesterday."

"That's amazing." Ella beamed at her.

"We didn't go out for very long, though." Amelie sighed. "Monty tried to chase a pigeon and Dad tripped over and nearly trod on Daisy."

"So does Monty get on with Daisy OK?" Ella asked. "He wasn't being naughty because he's jealous of you fussing over her?"

"Of course not! Anyway, I don't

fuss over Daisy more than I do over him." *Well, maybe a little more,* a small voice inside her said. *But I have to – she's been so upset...* Amelie shook her head firmly. "Monty's fine. How's your project going? Did your mum help you with the sewing?"

She was glad when Ella rolled her eyes and started telling her about the dress disaster she was having. That little voice was still niggling away inside Amelie, telling her that maybe she had been neglecting Monty a bit...

Everyone in the class was excited about their projects – Miss Garrett said she was going to send a note home inviting parents in to see them all on Friday after school. Amelie was determined that her mosaic was going to be perfect. She had printed out a picture of a real Roman mosaic from the Internet – an under the sea scene with all sorts of fish. Amelie had decided to make just one big fish, otherwise it would take too long. Dad had gone to the craft shop and got her a big sheet of card and lots of colours of foam. It had taken ages to cut out all the little squares but now she just had to finish sticking them on top of the colour printout.

When she got home from school she laid out her box with all the coloured squares on the kitchen table and started to stick them down along the delicate arched fin on the fish's back – it was almost the last bit. She was so focused on the task that she didn't notice Monty getting up out of his basket.

The puppy had been sleeping off his dinner but he woke up feeling bright and bouncy, and spotted Amelie sitting at the kitchen table at once. He wanted her to fuss over him – or, even better, take him for a walk. He'd had a quick run with Dad that morning but he'd been in the house most of the day and Amelie hadn't taken him out when she got back from school.

Monty laid his muzzle in Amelie's lap, gazing up at her with round, hopeful eyes. He expected her to reach down and stroke his ears, like she usually did.

Instead Amelie squealed and jumped – she'd been concentrating so hard, she hadn't heard Monty coming. She caught the box of foam squares with her elbow and it went flying, pieces of foam scattering everywhere.

Monty skittered backwards. He didn't like the tiny pieces, and he snapped and clawed at them as they fell on his nose and ears.

"Oh no, Monty. Stop it!" Amelie grabbed his collar but Monty pulled away and accidentally barged into the table. Amelie's glass of water tipped over, spilling right across her picture.

"My mosaic!" Amelie wailed, letting go of Monty and trying to snatch the mosaic out of the way. But it was too late – the water had gone all over it.

"Look what you've done! Monty, you bad dog!" Amelie yelled.

Monty wriggled backwards across the kitchen, crouching low and watching Amelie out of the corner of his eye. He didn't understand what he had done but he could tell that she was angry.

There was a thumping of footsteps on the stairs and Dad hurried in. "What's the matter?"

"Look!" Amelie sniffed, wiping her hand across her eyes.

"Oh dear…" Dad picked up the mosaic, trying to brush off the worst of the water. "How did that happen?"

"Monty bumped the table," Amelie said crossly. "It's ruined. The card's going all wrinkly."

"I reckon we can rescue it." Dad looked at the mosaic thoughtfully. "I'll get your mum to pick up some more card on her way home. We can cut out the bits you've already stuck down and put them on that." He swept the stray pieces of foam into his hand. "I'll help but first I've got to finish packing for this trip tomorrow. Why don't you help me squash everything into my bag and we'll work on it later, OK?"

Amelie nodded and followed him upstairs, leaving Monty in the kitchen, gazing sadly after them. He didn't remember Amelie ever shouting at him like that before. He ducked his head as Daisy got out of her basket and came to sniff at a couple of craft-foam pieces that Dad had missed. Then she pattered over to him, her tail gently wagging. Monty licked at his muzzle nervously but Daisy didn't snap at him this time. Instead she gave his nose a friendly lick. Monty leaned down, nudging at her gratefully with his muzzle. Finally, somebody who wasn't cross with him!

Daisy trotted back to her basket and lay down but she kept glancing over at Monty. He stared back at her uncertainly. He wanted to lie down in his basket, where he felt safe, but he wanted to stay close to Daisy, too. It was the friendliest she'd ever been and she was making him feel better.

Monty crouched down at the side of his basket and pushed it with his nose across the kitchen tiles until it was next to Daisy's. Then he scrambled in and buried his head down the side of the cushion. He could hear her breathing peacefully next to him as he fell asleep.

Chapter Five

"Morning, Amelie! Time to wake up."

Amelie peered up at her mum. "Has Dad gone?" she asked, through a yawn.

"Yes, he had to get up at four to get to the airport." Mum sighed. "I'm just going to make your packed lunches, OK?" She hurried out of the room and Amelie heard her trotting down the stairs. Usually Dad did all the school things, like their packed lunches and making sure Amelie remembered her football kit on the right days.

Amelie climbed out of bed, and then jumped as she heard a cry and a loud yelp from downstairs. "What is it?" she called anxiously, running out to lean over the banisters.

"It's that silly puppy! He's moved his basket across the kitchen and I tripped over it. Don't worry. Monty's fine – he's just surprised."

Amelie dashed downstairs to check on the puppy. Monty had sounded really panicked. He was sitting in his basket, watching Mum nervously.

"He was a bit scared by me yelling," Mum admitted. "But I didn't expect his basket to be there! I was rushing about trying to find the juice cartons for your lunch and I tripped. Oh dear… He doesn't look happy."

"Poor Monty." Amelie went over and crouched next to his basket, stroking the puppy's head. Monty licked her arm lovingly and Amelie smiled. But then she looked up and saw her mosaic, still drying on the counter. In the end Dad had said it would be best to wait before cutting it up and trying to rescue it.

Amelie sighed. It hadn't really been Monty's fault but her mosaic was never going to be as good second time round. She couldn't help feeling cross with him. She stood up sharply, pulling her hand away from him. Monty stared after her in surprise.

"I'll help you stick it back together," Josh said, coming into the kitchen and seeing her scowling at the ruined mosaic.

"Thanks." Amelie gave him a quick hug. "Mum, did you feed Monty and Daisy?"

Monty stood up in his basket, his tail wagging hopefully. He'd heard his name.

Mum shook her head. "Not yet. Sorry, dogs."

"It's OK, I'll do it." Amelie picked up both the bowls and put them on the counter, ready to pour out the dry food. Now that Monty and Daisy were more used to each other, they didn't have to eat at opposite ends of the kitchen.

Monty scampered over, eager for his breakfast. Daisy heard the dry biscuits rattling into her bowl and erupted out of her basket, ears flapping. Amelie giggled – Daisy was so funny. She was just about to put the bowls down when Monty reached over her arm and tried to gobble a mouthful. He was so hungry he stuck his nose in the wrong bowl and Amelie pulled it away.

"No—" she started to say but Daisy got there first. She snapped angrily at Monty and he darted back in fright, his ears flattening and his tail tucking between his legs.

"Daisy!" Mum cried. She took the food bowls out of Amelie's hands and put them down on the floor. "Are you all right, Amelie?"

"Yes… She wasn't anywhere near me – she was cross with Monty because he was trying to nick her food. She didn't actually bite me. Or Monty." Amelie's voice shook a little. Monty had chewed at her fingers sometimes when he was little but he'd never come close to biting. She could see why Daisy had been upset but it was still scary.

"Well, at least Monty's not hurt," Mum said. "And Daisy's forgotten about it already, look. She's eating her breakfast."

Amelie nodded. Daisy was wolfing down her food – so different to that first day when they'd brought her back from Grandad's. "I suppose she's never had to share…"

Monty had retreated to his basket again. He was hungry but he didn't want to eat next to Daisy, not after she'd snapped at him like that. Everything seemed to be going wrong. Amelie was angry with him, Mum had shouted and now Daisy had gone back to being unfriendly. He watched Amelie and Josh eating breakfast, hoping that someone would come and make a fuss of him but they were rushing to get off to school.

Quietly, he crept out of his basket and over to the kitchen door. He didn't feel like being inside any more, where everyone was cross. He slipped through the dog flap and padded down to the end of the garden to look out through the wire fence.

The field was empty, apart from a flock of starlings. Monty stood there, wagging his tail uncertainly as they hopped across the long grass. But he didn't feel like barking at them and they didn't pay any attention to the small black dog on the other side of the fence.

Monty lay curled up next to the fence, watching the comings and goings on the field. It was much busier now, with dogs going for walks. There were a few young children running about as well. Monty watched the other dogs enviously as they raced around. If only he could go for a good run like that. That little boy might even let him chase his ball.

Monty pressed his nose closer to the fence and whined, wishing the little boy would kick his ball closer. He scrabbled at the wire with one paw and then jumped back as the fence moved. It was loose at the bottom. There'd been no rain for a while and the dry, dusty earth had worn away. There was *almost* a hole.

Monty sniffed at it curiously and then scratched at the earth, sending dust flying. He whisked back, sneezing and shaking his head. The hole was bigger, definitely. This time he put his nose down and tried to squeeze it under the fence. It was tight but the wire was curling up at the bottom, and if he wriggled and pushed and scrabbled some more with his paws…

Suddenly, to his surprise, Monty shot out on the other side. He was in the field!

There was a scurry of paws behind him and a sharp warning bark. Monty looked back at the fence and saw that Daisy was there. She didn't sound angry – more confused. Maybe even a little bit frightened.

He wagged his tail at her, trying to show that everything was all right. Now that he was out in the field, with the sun warming his fur and all the delicious smells to explore, he didn't mind that she'd snapped at him.

With a friendly bark, Monty crouched down, stretching out his front paws, inviting Daisy to come and play. Perhaps she could wriggle under the fence, too? Then they could chase each other through the long grass. But Daisy only stood there and barked again. Monty looked back and forth a few times, between Daisy and that exciting stretch of grass. Then he turned his back on her and darted off into the field.

Chapter Six

Monty pottered about, catching the scents of other dogs. Then a flash of movement caught his eye – the little boy with the ball. He was kicking it about, giggling and stumbling over the long grass.

Monty trotted up to him, and crouched down hopefully, asking the little boy to play. But the boy didn't understand. He just stared at the puppy, his eyes wide. Monty barked encouragingly, hoping that the boy would throw the ball but he didn't. He backed away a couple of steps, looking nervous. In the distance, the boy's mother heard the barking. She put his baby sister down in the pushchair and began to run towards them.

Monty barked again but the boy still didn't throw the ball to him. Instead he turned and tried to run away but in his fright he tripped up and fell sprawling in the grass. He let out a wail and Monty eyed him worriedly. That wasn't a good noise. Cautiously he padded closer and by the time the boy's mother came running up, Monty was standing over him.

"Leave him alone! Go away!"

Monty stepped back, tucking his tail between his legs. Why was she shouting? He'd only wanted to play. He licked his muzzle anxiously and then flinched as the mum swiped at him with the baby's teddy.

She didn't actually hit Monty but he yelped in surprise. What was going on? Now somebody else was shouting at him. He backed away, whimpering, but the frightened mum kept shouting, "Leave him! Bad dog!" and the little boy was still crying and then the baby joined in, too…

Monty turned and ran. He hadn't meant to hurt anyone and he didn't understand what he'd done wrong. All he knew was that he had to get away.

"Can we take the dogs out when we get back?" Amelie asked Josh on her way home from school. Because Dad was away and Mum was still at work, her brother had picked her up.

Josh nodded. "Yeah. Good idea. I bet Monty'd love a proper run."

Amelie was expecting Monty to come rushing up when they opened the front door – and maybe Daisy, too. But there was no patter of paws. The house was silent.

"Where are they?" she asked. Monty always came to see her as soon as she got back from school. Why wasn't he waiting for her by the door?

Amelie sighed, feeling guilty.

Maybe what Ella had hinted at was true – Monty was upset that they had a new dog. She hadn't been paying him as much attention as she usually did because she'd been worrying about Daisy. *I need to show Monty I still love him...* she thought to herself.

She hurried through the kitchen to the back door, her fingers slipping and fumbling as she tried to turn the key. As she stepped outside, she expected Monty to come running up to her – but the garden seemed to be completely empty. She ran down the path, calling, "Monty! Where are you? Daisy? Come on! Here!" She could hear Josh hurrying after her and calling, too.

Then at last Amelie saw a flash of

colour down at the end of the garden – Daisy's reddish-brown fur. The little dog came trotting up to them, wagging her tail.

Amelie patted Daisy's head but she only had half an eye on the dachshund. She still couldn't see Monty anywhere. He wasn't the sort of dog you didn't notice. She couldn't just have missed him. He wasn't there…

"Josh, I've found Daisy – look! But where's Monty?"

"He has to be here somewhere," Josh said, staring around the garden. "Maybe he's asleep under a bush…"

"But he always wakes up and comes to see us when we get home!" Amelie pointed out, her voice squeaky with panic.

"Don't stress, Amelie. I'll go and
check inside. Maybe he got shut in one
of the bedrooms or something." Josh
ran back up the garden, and Amelie
began to search up and down the lawn.

"Perhaps he went into one of the
gardens next door," Amelie suggested,
as Josh came back out, shaking his
head. "What if there's a gap in the
fence?" She stepped into the flower bed,
peering between the plants. "I can't see

any holes," she told Josh doubtfully.

"None on this side, either," he agreed. "I think we'd better call Mum – maybe she left the front door open for a minute when she went to work?"

"She won't be able to answer, though," Amelie pointed out. "She can't have her phone on her when she's out in the shop, can she?"

"No, you're right. I'll just have to leave a message. Then I'll go up and down the street, and ask if anyone's seen him."

"Josh, what if Monty's been wandering the streets for hours?" Amelie whispered. "We don't know when he got out, do we? If Mum let him out by accident, he could be miles away by now."

"You stay here and check the fence again, just in case. I'll go and ask the neighbours." Josh sped back into the house and Amelie squeezed behind the plants to look at the fence properly. She got herself tangled in a rose bush and scratched her arm but she was too worried to notice it hurting.

"Where is he, Daisy?" Amelie said, as the dachshund came to stand next to her, peering at the fence, too. "Did you see him?" Then she blinked and looked down at Daisy, thinking hard. "Maybe you did see where he went? Daisy, where's Monty?"

Daisy gazed up at her with dark, serious eyes.

Amelie sighed. "I'm being stupid, aren't I? You're not a police dog or anything… You were probably asleep in your basket, anyway."

But then the little dachshund turned round and marched out of the flower bed, as though she actually was going to find him. Amelie gazed after her for a moment – and then she scrambled out between the bushes and raced down the garden.

Daisy was in the corner right at the end, between the sweet peas Mum was growing up the fence. Her nose was practically touching the wire.

Amelie looked at Daisy doubtfully. Perhaps she'd just got bored and wandered off – but it really had looked like she understood when Amelie said Monty's name. "He's not here, Daisy," she said.

Daisy
glanced up
at her and
then scrabbled at the fence with her
neat little paws, so that the dusty earth
went flying.

Amelie crouched down, pulling at
the fence and then caught her breath in
excitement. The wire mesh was loose!
It was coming away from the post at
the bottom and there was definitely
a bit of a hole there, too. A hole that
might have been dug out...

"Is that where he went?" Amelie
asked Daisy. She was so desperate to
know what had happened, she almost
felt like the little dog might answer her.

But Daisy only sniffed at the hole
again and then stared out at the field.

Chapter Seven

Monty shot through the gate into the main park, panting hard. His claws pattered on the tarmac path that led around the lake and he began to feel calmer. He knew this place. This was where he walked with Amelie. He liked to go sniffing along the little iron fence around the water. Amelie didn't mind – she'd stand for ages and

let him catch all the smells. Monty
stood resting his chin on the fence,
looking across the lake. He wanted
Amelie.

Monty huffed out a deep sigh and
then blinked as he heard a duck quack.
His tail twitched just a little from
side to side and he pushed
his muzzle through the
fence for a closer look.
There was a
whole line
of them
coming
his way,
marching
flatfooted
around the
bank.

Monty felt his tail twitch with excitement. He could scramble over the fence – or maybe even through the bars. Something deep down inside him wanted to jump the fence and run barking at the ducks so that they fluttered and flapped and quacked. But he knew he mustn't. Dad had shouted at him when he'd tried to catch that pigeon the day before.

He turned away from the fence, his head drooping. They were all cross with him. Everyone was. Even that woman had shouted at him – and he'd only been trying to play with the little boy with the ball. He trailed along the path, not sure where he was going. If he went back across the field to the garden fence, she might still

be there. He didn't want to go past
her again. And besides, everyone at
home was angry with him, too. Maybe
he shouldn't be going back there at
all? But he wanted to see Amelie and
Josh so much. He was hungry, too, he
realized. His stomach was growling –
it felt like a long time since he'd eaten.
Perhaps he *should* go home…

Monty stopped and sniffed. He
could smell food! He followed his
nose until he came to a scattering
of stale bread, piled up at the edge
of the path. He started to gobble it
down eagerly, even though it was old
and dry.

Then, suddenly, a huge creature was
there, too, snapping and hissing and
flapping its wings. Monty jumped back

with a growl of fright. It was a goose. He'd seen geese round the lake before. Amelie always pulled him away when they came stomping past.

Monty hated to be chased away from the food. He had found it first, after all! But the goose was enormous. And now there was another one coming and another.

They hissed and darted their beaks
at him until he backed away further.
He crouched under a bench, watching
as they ate up all of the bread. They
weren't going to leave any of it for him
and his stomach was still so empty.
Monty sagged down, resting
his chin on his paws and
gazed at them sadly.

"Josh, look! There *is* a hole! Daisy showed me."

Josh looked at the fence. "Monty couldn't get out through that. It's not big enough."

"But look, I think he dug underneath. See where the soil's all scratched away? And if he pushed this loose bit of fence, too…"

Josh shook his head. "I still reckon Mum must have let him out the front by accident. But no one's seen him – I've asked the neighbours on both sides. I think I ought to go and look for him along the next couple of streets. Can you stay here, Amelie? In case the phone rings? It's the home number on his collar – someone might find him and call. I just checked the answering machine and there aren't any messages yet but people will be coming home from work now. He might be in somebody's garden."

"All right." Amelie nodded, getting up to follow Josh into the house. "Come on, Daisy."

But Daisy didn't follow her. Amelie glanced up the garden at the house as Josh disappeared inside. She was about to go and leave Daisy behind but something held her back. The dachshund was still sniffing at the hole and looking out at the field. As Amelie watched, she clawed at the fence, pulling it back a little. There was definitely a space, even with only

Daisy's small paws working at it. Monty would have been able to pull a lot harder, Amelie thought.

"He did go out that way, didn't he?" she muttered to Daisy. She glanced uncertainly back up the garden. What if someone called, like Josh had said? But they could leave a message, after all… Amelie bit her lip, peering through the wire at the field. Daisy obviously thought Monty was out there somewhere. Maybe she could even help Amelie to find him? Amelie couldn't lose this chance – although she knew she wasn't allowed to go to the park on her own.

"I'll be back soon, I promise," she whispered, looking back towards the house. Even though Josh wasn't actually there, she felt as though she ought to explain.

Amelie nodded her head firmly. She *had* to go. She was sure that Monty had run off because of the way she'd treated him. She'd been making such a big fuss of Daisy that he must have felt like she didn't love him any more. And then she'd been so grumpy about her project!

"Daisy, stay!" Amelie dashed back into the house, grabbing Daisy's lead and then Monty's as well. Because she *was* going to find him. Then she ran back down the garden. The dachshund was clawing at the fence again, her tail wagging briskly from side to side. But she let Amelie clip on her lead.

Amelie pulled the loose edge of the fence back as far as she could and

crouched down, watching as Daisy
darted through the gap. Then she
wriggled after the dog. The gap where
the fence had come away from the
post was easily big enough for Daisy,
and even Monty, but it was tight for a
nine-year-old girl. The loose edges of
the wire caught in Amelie's hair and
she panicked for a moment, sure she
was stuck. Then, with a huge pull, she
was free, collapsing on to the grass.

Amelie stood up, rubbing at the
sore patch where her hair had pulled.
"Come on, Daisy. I'm sure he's out
here somewhere. Monty!"

Amelie had been racing all over the
field for what seemed liked hours, with
Daisy leaping in and out of the clumps
of grass. She wasn't feeling nearly so
certain now. There were quite a few
other dogs out with their owners and
Amelie had even seen a black Labrador.
For a second her stomach had jumped
with excitement and then she realized
that the Lab was far too big.

Now they were hurrying round
the lake and Amelie was peering

along the banks. She was pretty sure that Monty was too big to squeeze through the bars of the little fence – but then she hadn't expected him to escape out of their garden, either.

"Sorry, Daisy," Amelie muttered. The dachshund was plodding along now, panting heavily. But she hadn't stopped, the way Amelie had seen her do with Grandad. Normally if she got tired on a walk she'd sit down solidly and sulk until someone carried her. Daisy seemed to be just as keen to keep looking as Amelie was.

"Monty doesn't like the lake as much as the field," Amelie said, crouching down for a moment to rub Daisy's silky ears. "But he likes watching the ducks. Maybe he did come this way. Oh, I just don't know! And we've been out for ages, Josh must have got back by now…"

She stood up, looking back and forth between the lake path and the opening in the hedge that led back to the field. What should they do?

"Just a quick look," she said to Daisy at last. "We can't give up yet, we just can't. Monty ran away because of me and now I've got bring him home."

Chapter Eight

Monty lay huddled under the bench in the shady patch where a huge buddleia bush had started to grow over the seat. The geese had gone now but he hadn't come out of his hiding place. It seemed better to stay where he was, even though he was so hungry. He let out a great, heavy sigh and wriggled on the dusty tarmac until he was a bit more comfortable. He was tired after all that running and the fright from the geese. The bees buzzing in the purple flowers over his head were making him feel sleepy, too…

Monty had almost drifted off when he heard them. The busy clicking of little clawed paws and Amelie's voice calling. Calling *him*!

"Monty! Monty! Here, boy!"

They were just a bit further round the path. Monty shook his head sleepily and almost leaped out from under the bench. But then he woke up a little more and something stopped him. Amelie had been so cross before – maybe he shouldn't go to her. But he *wanted* to! He shuffled forwards uncertainly, peering out between the branches. He wanted Amelie to pat him and pull his ears that special way she did and tell him he was a good boy. But what if she didn't? Daisy was with Amelie, too – and Amelie never seemed to be cross with *her*.

Monty whined – he just didn't know what to do. But then he heard Amelie calling again and something in her voice made him scramble out from under the bench. He didn't care if she was still cross. He had to go back to her.

He was shaking the dust and bits of twig out of his fur when he saw them running towards him, Daisy trotting ahead with her tail wagging eagerly and Amelie hurrying after her. Monty looked up at Amelie, uncertain but hopeful, his tail beating slowly from side to side.

"Oh, Monty! We were so worried about you!" Amelie crouched down beside him and brushed a bit of dirt off his nose. "Please don't ever do that again."

Her voice was trembling and Monty eyed her uncertainly. She didn't sound angry with him but she didn't sound like her usual self, either. He nosed at her hand and she laughed. "We didn't know where you were," she whispered,

running her hand over his head over
and over again. "I was so scared. I'm
sorry I was grumpy with you. It wasn't
your fault about my project. I know
you just wanted me to fuss over you
like I'd been fussing over Daisy."

Monty sat down and leaned against
her knees,
loving the
soothing
murmur of
her voice.

"I bet you're starving," Amelie
said suddenly. "Monty, do you want
dinner?" She giggled as he jumped up,
his tail wagging like mad. "That'll be a
yes, then. Oh, and we should get back
and tell Josh we've found you!" She
clipped on Monty's lead and hurried
the two dogs back round the lake
towards the gate that led out to the
alleyway.

Amelie rang the front doorbell
in one long peal. Then she peered
through the glass, trying to see her
brother coming to answer the door.

"I'm behind you!"

Amelie jumped round to find Josh
running up the path, grinning at her.

"You found him! Where was he?
Wow, Monty, I've been looking all

over for you!" He crouched down to stroke the puppy, while Monty whined delightedly and scrabbled at his knees. Josh fussed over him for a moment and then looked up at Amelie, frowning. "Hang on! You're supposed to be in the house in case someone phones! Where have you been?"

Amelie folded her arms and glared. "I got him back, Josh! He *had* gone out through that hole in the fence – he was in the park. Daisy was right…" Then she spotted Monty's anxious eyes and softened her voice. "I know I shouldn't have gone on my own."

Josh sighed. "At least he's home. I'd better leave Mum another message. I don't know what I'm going to tell her, though."

"I really am sorry, Josh. Daisy was so sure. She pulled the fence up with her paw and I was certain she knew where Monty had gone. I didn't want to miss the chance of finding him."

Josh nodded and pulled out his keys. "I won't say anything to Mum. But don't ever do anything like that again, OK?"

Monty barked encouragingly as the keys jangled and Daisy gave an excited little yap.

"Yes, all right, you both want dinner. Come on then!" Josh unlocked the door and the two dogs rushed in, jumping around Amelie's feet while she tried to take off their leads.

"I'll get the food ready," Josh called, heading into the kitchen. "Amelie, just look at Daisy. Think back to a week ago!"

Amelie beamed as she finally managed to unclip the lead from Daisy's collar and the dachshund licked her cheek. "I know," she said, following the two dogs into the kitchen. "But I feel really bad, Josh. I was worrying so much about her I forgot about Monty. He thought no one loved him any more."

Josh put the food bowls down – side by side – and watched as the two dogs tucked in. They didn't look bothered about eating right next to each other at all. "I guess you're probably right," he admitted. "We did neglect him – even though we didn't mean to."

Monty licked out the last crumbs

from his food bowl, cleaning it so thoroughly that it went scraping across the floor. He looked at it for a moment, in case some more food suddenly appeared – and then he yawned so widely that Amelie could see every one of his teeth. He gave the bowl one last sniff and padded wearily over to his basket, climbing in and slumping down.

Daisy inspected her bowl and then pattered across the tiles after him. Their baskets were still next to each other but she didn't climb into hers at once. She stood there, looking at Monty, who was lying with his nose hanging out over the side of his huge basket. Daisy came a little closer and then hopped in with him, curling up in front of Monty's tummy.

Amelie held her breath. Monty lifted up his head to stare at Daisy and he seemed a bit surprised but he didn't look as though he minded. He laid his head down again and lifted one long black paw, draping it lovingly over Daisy's side.

"He's hugging her!" Amelie whispered.

Josh pulled out his phone to take a picture. "I'm sending this one to Grandad."

"She's like a different dog," Grandad said, smiling at Amelie. "Having a puppy like Monty to play with has taken years off her. Look at her go!"

Amelie nodded. Daisy was galloping down the garden towards them, chasing Monty, who had a rubber bone in his mouth.

"She's hardly touching the ground," Amelie giggled. "Look at her flappy ears! I think she's going to take off."

Monty skidded up to them and dropped the bone in front of Amelie, who was sitting by Grandad's feet.

"You're so clever!" Amelie rubbed his nose. "Shall I throw it again? Are you going to let Daisy fetch it this time?" She waved the bone at him and then threw it down the garden. Monty hurled himself after it.

"Ha!" Grandad laughed. "Daisy's got a strategy. She's not coming all the way back up here, she's waiting halfway so she can get to it first. Daisy, that's cheating!"

"She's allowed to cheat a bit," Mum pointed out, handing Grandad a mug of tea.

Josh reached over to grab a glass of juice from the tray. "Yeah, look how much shorter her legs are."

"Don't you miss her, Grandad?" Amelie asked suddenly. Then she wished she hadn't – she didn't want to make Grandad sad. But she couldn't imagine giving up Monty and she'd only had him for a few months. Daisy had been Grandad's dog for years.

"Of course I do." Grandad sighed. "But I wasn't taking her on enough walks, Amelie. She's better off here. I'm really settled in my new flat and there are people around to look after me if I need it but I still get to see Daisy. It's the best of both worlds."

"It's been brilliant for Monty, too," Amelie said, smiling as Daisy whipped the bone out from under Monty's nose. "He loves having her to play with, especially when we're at school."

Mum nodded. "I think we might have to get a bigger basket. Daisy never sleeps in hers any more and Monty's growing so fast they won't both fit in his soon."

Daisy hurtled up the garden towards them and dropped the bone triumphantly next to Grandad's feet. Then she sat down between him and Amelie, panting heavily and looking delighted with herself.

Monty trotted up to them and nudged his nose against Daisy's. Then he slumped down on Amelie's other side, resting his head on her bare feet. He didn't mind about not getting to the bone first – not that much – but he wanted everyone to know that Amelie belonged to him.

Amelie giggled as the whiskery underside of his muzzle tickled her toes. "You're such a good boy, Monty," she whispered. "You know that, don't you?"

HOLLY WEBB

Holly Webb started out as a children's book editor, and wrote her first series for the publisher she worked for. She has been writing ever since, with over one hundred books to her name. Holly lives in Berkshire, with her husband and three young sons. Holly's pet cats are always nosying around when she is trying to type on her laptop.

For more information
about Holly Webb visit:

www.holly-webb.com